BOOK FOUR

A Story About Respecting Others

Miss Marbles's Marvelous Makeover

by SHEILA WALSH

illustrations by DON SULLIVAN

 A CHILDREN OF FAITH BOOK *published by* WATERBROOK PRESS

MISS MARBLES'S MARVELOUS MAKEOVER
PUBLISHED BY WATERBROOK PRESS
2375 Telstar Drive, Suite 160
Colorado Springs, Colorado 80920
A division of Random House, Inc.

ISBN 1-57856-338-0

Published in association with the literary agency of Alive Communications, Inc.,
7680 Goddard Street, Suite 200, Colorado Springs, CO 80920.

 The executive producer of Gnoo Zoo is Stephen Arterburn, M.Ed.
Children of Faith, 402 BNA Drive, Suite 600, Nashville, TN 37217

Printed in the United States of America
2001—First Edition

10 9 8 7 6 5 4 3 2 1

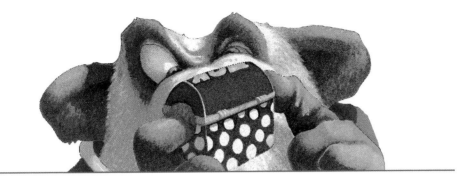

"We forgive you for eating your hammer," Big Billy said to Einstein. "But how will we ever open this box now? The True Gnoo Key is inside!"

"You must journey once more to find the Great White Tiger," Lulu said. "The Snowkeeper will show you the way." She pointed to a small house on the mountainside below. Then with a flick of her tail, she was gone.

Big Billy steered the hot-air balloon toward the Snowkeeper's house.

—*Einstein's Enormous Error*

"Be careful, Big Billy!" Miss Marbles whined as her friend tried to lower the tiny basket to the ground in the strong wind. "I'm a little queasy and a trifle sneezy. When this is all over I will definitely need to recline in the sun!"

The basket finally landed with a soft thud in the snow.

"Ah, land, glorious land!" Miss Marbles said.

"Perhaps we'll have time for a bit of skiing?" Einstein suggested as he tried to climb out of the basket.

"Focus, focus!" Miss Marbles said. She stood up tall and proud. "We are on a mission that only *we* can fulfill."

"Now, now!" Big Billy said. "Let's remember we can do nothing without the Great White Tiger."

"Yes, but he did choose us for the job," Miss Marbles replied.

The group made their way toward the Snowkeeper's hut.

"Wow! Hello! Not working for me!" Chattaboonga cried as she sank into the snow.

"Mfn effner!" Boongachatta's muffled voice came from a snowdrift.

Einstein fished out the sisters and carried them to the Snowkeeper's door.

"Allow me!" Miss Marbles said, lifting her wing to knock.

A small round penguin opened the door.

"Ah, good day, my fellow earthbound bird," Miss Marbles began.

"Silence!" the Snowkeeper said.

"Well! How rude!"

"Silence I say! Come inside quickly," the penguin commanded. "And guard that box. You have been followed."

Everyone except Miss Marbles hurried in. "Well, I don't see anyone," she said, "and I certainly don't take orders from a rude bird who can't even walk in a straight li—oh!"

The Snowkeeper grabbed Miss Marbles's pearls and yanked her inside.

"There is no time to waste," the Snowkeeper said, taking some backpacks off a shelf. "Put on these parachutes."

"Can you direct us to the Great White Tiger, sir?" Big Billy asked.

"I will. But hurry," he said. "Evil is overhead."

"Evil, schmeevil," Miss Marbles muttered.

"Silence, foolish bird," the Snowkeeper said. "Lives are at stake."

Miss Marbles threw down her pack and stomped her foot. "Just a little courtesy to one's fellow feathered friends would be ni—!"

A thundering *boom!* cut her off, and Reptillion and Creepshaw burst through the roof.

"It is too late for you now, proud one!" the Snowkeeper cried. He pulled a lever, and a huge trapdoor opened beneath the group.

"Pull your cords—now!" he cried.

Everybody pulled as they fell into the darkness below. Everybody except Miss Marbles, that is.

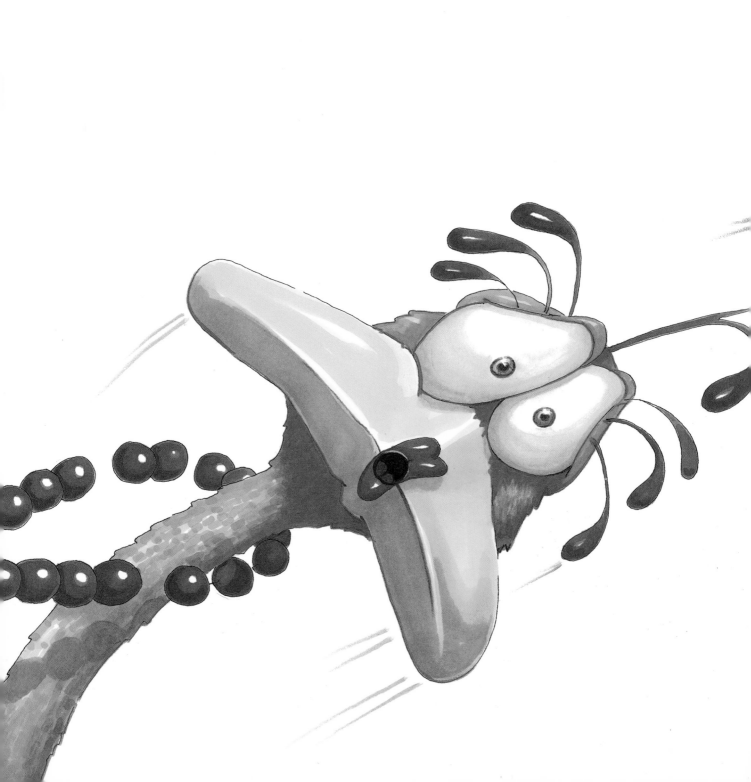

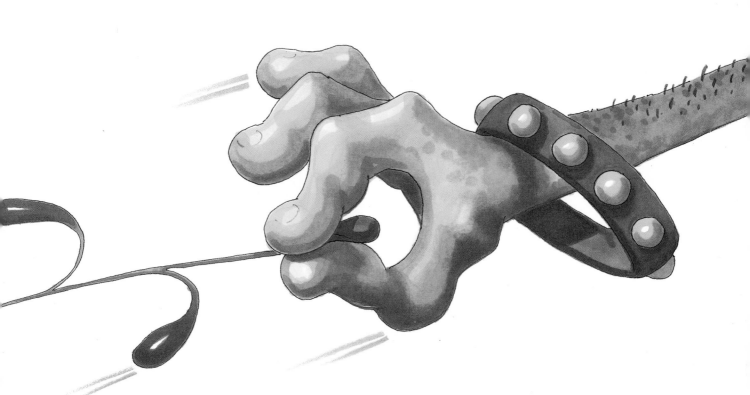

Miss Marbles clung to the edge of the open hole. "Oh, my goodness! Oh, nice snowbirdie! Help!"

"At your service," Reptillion said as he grabbed Miss Marbles. An enormous black raven swooped down and lifted them out into the darkening sky.

"Big Billy! Einstein! Don't leave me!" Miss Marbles cried.

"It's too late, birdbrain," Reptillion growled. "They're long gone. But we'll take you instead!"

The sky grew dark as they flew into a storm, through miles and miles of clouds and rain.

"Great White Tiger, can you still see me?" Miss Marbles whimpered. A jagged fork of lightning struck close by.

"Release us!" Reptillion finally cried. The giant bird swooped toward the earth.

"Whoa! Delicate stomach here!" said Creepshaw.

The bird set them down on the bank of a fast and furious river.

"Now, dear girl," Reptillion began. "Tell me: Where are your friends taking the box that holds the True Gnoo Key?"

"I...I...I don't know," Miss Marbles whispered.

"I think you do!" he said. Creepshaw plucked one of her feathers.

"Ouch! Oh dear, I don't! We were hoping the Great Whi—"

"Aahhrrggh!" Reptillion roared to the sky. "Do not speak that name! If you don't know, then I am finished with you!"

With a massive blow he sent Miss Marbles into the turbulent water.

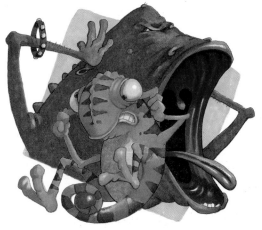

"After her! That fat cat she loves will save her. Then we'll find the key!"

Miss Marbles fluttered and sputtered in the rushing river. "Great White Tiger!" she cried. "You are my only hope! You can hear me anywhere. Help me now!"

Faster and faster the water carried her toward a bottomless waterfall. She closed her eyes.

Just as her toes slipped over the edge, something lifted her high into the air.

A familiar *bark! bark!* filled her ears.

"Lou! Is that you?" she cried.

"You got it, sister," Lou growled. "Sit tight!"

They flew out of the storm and into the sunlight, landing at last on a smooth, warm stone.

"I've ruined everything," Miss Marbles cried. "All because I didn't want to take orders from a bird smaller than I. What a silly girl I am."

"Sometimes truth comes from strange sources, lady," Lou said. "So you gotta learn to listen for it with Gnoo ears. The Snowkeeper knew you were in danger 'cause it won't be long before you get that box open."

"My pride is a terrible thing, Lou. Now I have lost my friends and I have lost my way."

"Well, lookee here," Lou said.

"I don't believe it!" she cried. Big Billy, Einstein, Chattaboonga, Boongachatta, and the Snowkeeper were sailing down through the clouds on their parachutes.

"How did you get here first, Miss Marbles?" Big Billy shouted.

"How did you get here at all?" Einstein added.

"And why are you so wet?" Chattaboonga chipped in.

For the first time in her life, Miss Marbles didn't know what to say.

"Time is nothin' to the Great White Tiger," Lou said to her with a wink.

Suddenly the Great White Tiger's gentle laughter filled the air.

Miss Marbles turned to see his magnificent wings outstretched to hug her.

"Forgive me, Snowkeeper," she cried. "Forgive me, Great White Tiger. Next time I will follow directions from anyone who serves you—even a bug! Even a really ugly bug!"

The Great White Tiger's laughter filled the air. "All right, my child. It is time to open this box!"

And at the touch of his silver-tipped paws, the box fell open.

"More than an ugly bug will be waiting for you next time!"

Inside was the most beautiful key anyone had ever seen. The True Gnoo Key. The key that would free all the animals held captive at the Gnoo Zoo.

"It is time to take this to the Gnoo Zoo, where it belongs," the Great White Tiger said.

"How will we get back?" Big Billy asked.

"You must cross the Sea of Glass," the Great White Tiger told him.

> *"When the sea seems gentle,*
> *take most care,*
> *for the Holes of Rooblesteen are there."*

Slowly and silently, before their very eyes, a glassy sea arose out of the ground.

"Let's go!" Miss Marbles said.

"Yes, let's go!" they all cried.

Learn how Einstein and his friends began their journey and met the Great White Tiger in Book One of the Gnoo Zoo series, *In Search of the Great White Tiger.*

In Book Two, *Chattaboonga's Chilling Choice,* the mischievous chimp would rather trust her instincts than the Great White Tiger's promises. She must learn the hard way that even when she is afraid, the Great White Tiger is always with the little band of travelers, and he will faithfully protect them on the journey.

In Gnoo Zoo Book Three, *Einstein's Enormous Error,* Einstein's love of chocolate causes real trouble and nearly sabotages the mission. Bickering and blaming each other for their problems, the friends must come to understand the value of forgiveness before they can find the True Gnoo Key.

More Gnoo Zoo and Children of Faith products are coming soon!